The Lord Is My Shepherd

Illustrated by
Anne Wilson

Eerdmans Books for Young Readers

Grand Rapids, Michigan   Cambridge, U.K.

The Lord is my shepherd;
I shall not want.

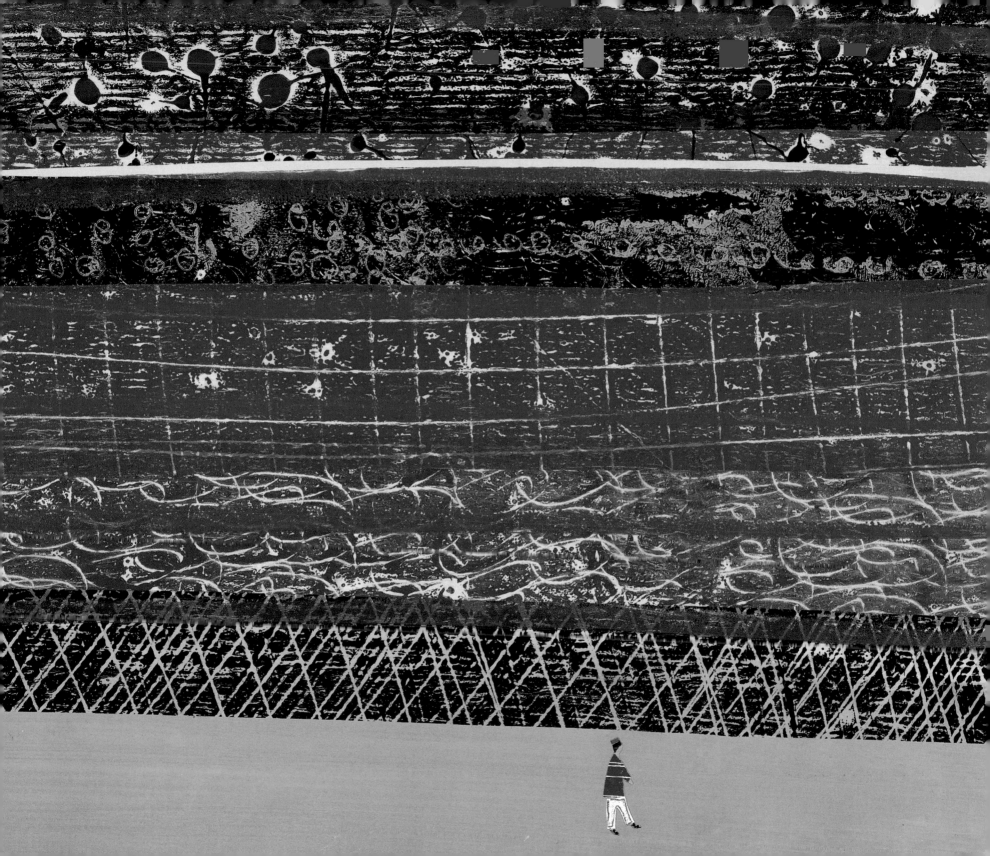

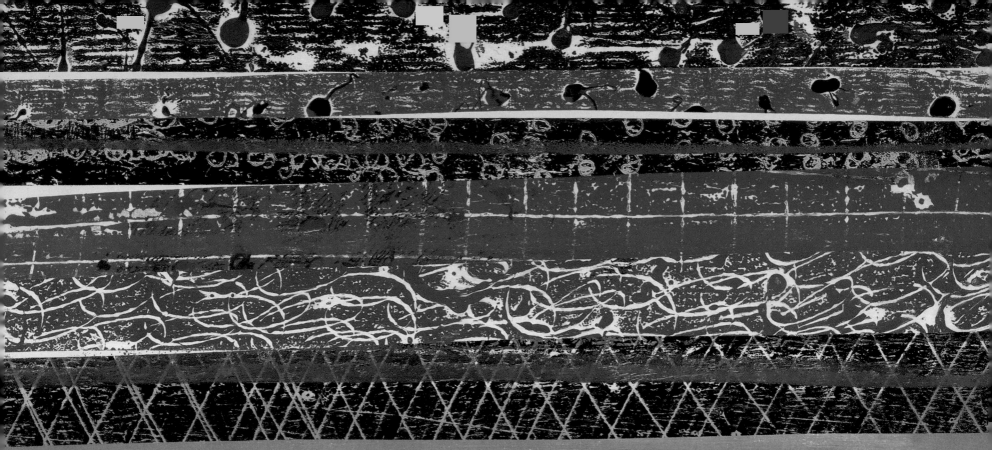

This edition published in 2003 by Eerdmans Books for Young Readers
an imprint of Wm B. Eerdmans Publishing Co.
255 Jefferson Ave. S.E.,
Grand Rapids, Michigan 49503
P.O. Box 163, Cambridge CB3 9PU U.K.

Created, designed, and produced by Tucker Slingsby Ltd,
Roebuck House, 288 Upper Richmond Road West,
London SW14 7JG

Printed in Singapore
Color reproduction by Bright Arts Graphics (Pte) Ltd, Singapore

1 2 3 4 5 6 7 8 9 08 07 06 05 04 03

Library of Congress Cataloging-in-Publication Data
Bible. O.T. Psalms XXIII. English. Authorized. 2003
The Lord is my shepherd / illustrated by Anne Wilson.
p. cm.
Summary: An illustrated version of the psalm which celebrates how the Lord meets the needs of His people.
ISBN 0-8028-5250-5 (alk. paper)
1. Bible. O.T. Psalms XXIII—Juvenile literature. [1. Bible. O.T. Psalms XXIII.] I. Wilson, Anne, 1974- ill. II. Title.
BS1450 23rd 2003
223'.2052034—dc21
2002010148

He maketh me

to lie down

in green pastures:

He leadeth me beside the still waters.

He restoreth
my soul:

for his name's sake.

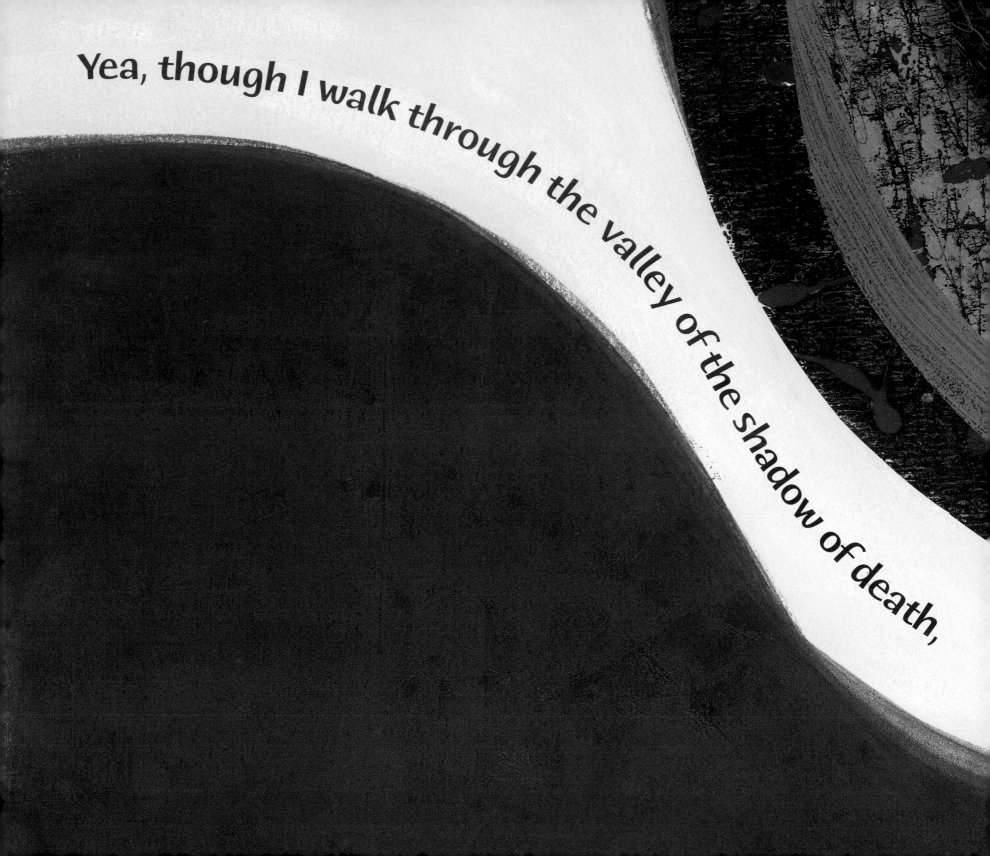

Yea, though I walk through the valley of the shadow of death,

I will fear no evil: for thou art with me;

Thy rod and thy staff they comfort me.

Thou preparest a table before me

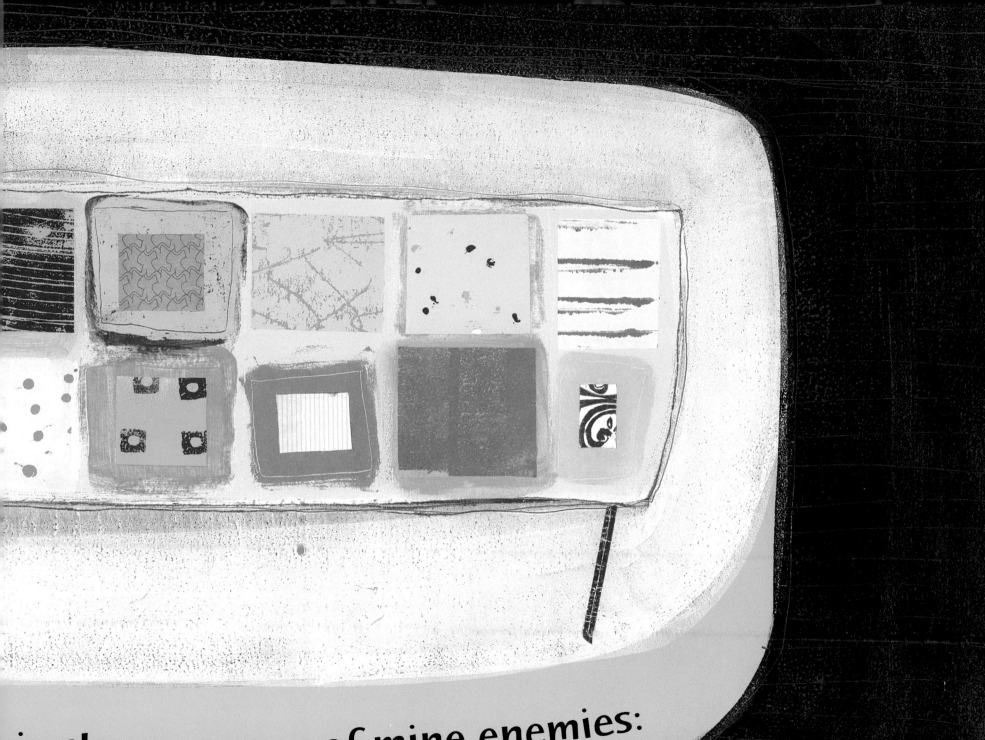

in the presence of mine enemies:

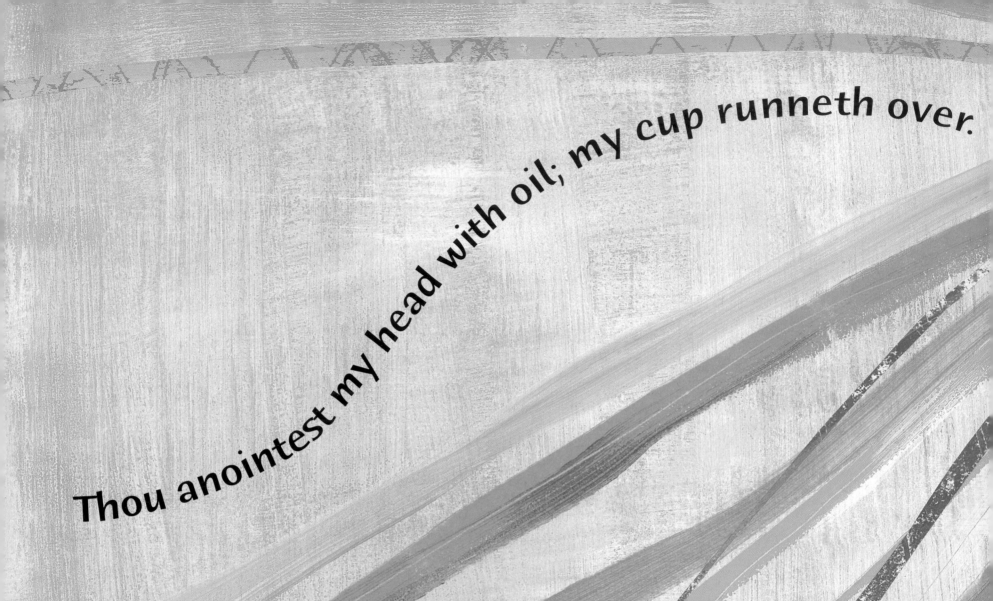

Thou anointest my head with oil; my cup runneth over.

Surely goodness and mercy shall follow me all the days of my life:

And I will dwell in the house of the Lord forever.